PREACHERS

BY AMOS YORK JR.

I0532723

©2016 Printed in the United States of America

Dedication

For

Dee York,

"Two brothers, one soul"

CONTENTS

FORWARD

At some point in our lives we have all experienced what it is like to be a part of a church ministry; the good and the bad. Whether in the capacity of being a loyal member, the pastor, a choir member, serving on the usher board, teaching bible study, being a deacon or in the case of this book's author, Amos York, Jr., as a "PK" preacher's kid.

We all have our perceptions of what church life should be verses what we actually see and experience, especially when it comes to the ministers, and in this book, "Preachers," you will get a glimpse into the lives of "church folks." Who better to deliver the untold stories than Amos ... And I'm not just saying that because he is my husband and an extraordinary writer... But because he lived through it first hand and his delivery is one that will leave you glued to the pages, laughing and gasping, wanting and waiting for more.

This funny, but very relatable tale of events, will either trigger memories and experiences of your own or it will transport you from the pages of the book into each church service, revival, and convocation leaving you feeling that you were physically there to experience all of the highs, lows, mess, fall outs, back-stabbing and most of all the very comical turn of events and situations.

It's very true that ministers are viewed as being superheroes... Invincible, honest, and free of wrong doing... But many forget that they are human and just like everyday people, they make mistakes, sometimes greater than you or I could ever imagine. In this book, Amos will show you just that, as well as how everyone around them can completely lose their minds all for the sake of the church.

I hope that you enjoy this fascinating journey through "Preachers" and that your experience is both humorous and life changing.

~ Twana M. York

INTRODUCTION

One of my favorite passages of scripture reads,
""Everyone who calls on the name of the Lord will be
saved." How then can they call on the One they have
not believed in? And how can they believe in the One
of whom they have not heard? And how can they hear
without someone to preach? And how can they preach
unless they are sent? As it is written: "How beautiful
are the feet of those who bring good news!" Romans
10: 13-15. That scripture alone is at the center of this
series of novels. All I've ever known was the church
and the voice of the Man of God better known as a
preacher. My entire young life was filled with so many
memories of the church.

The office of a preacher is akin to that of a king or some
other lofty position of leadership. In fact, a preacher

can be seen as the President of his own United States. He or she has unquestioned authority but also has the responsibility of being the voice of God himself. In the African-American community, the preacher has rock star status. We are taught to respect the office of the preacher. So many stories like the ones contained in these pages never get told as a result of such loyal followers. One of the worst things you can do is speak ill of a preacher.

My intent is to relay my point of view of the preachers that I encountered on my journey. These views are only stories that I gave narration to in my head. This is the church as I have imagined it to be during my formative years. There was an urge in me to write this novel since my teen-aged years but I never envisioned me completing my thoughts. Please venture with me as I attempt to give you a small piece of my gift of narration. I hope that you enjoy reading the first installment of this wonderful saga. It is my prayer that it reminds you of your preacher.

CHAPTER 1:

THE TRANSFORMATION

I owe everything that I am to the church. It has propelled me into the direction of my life's greatest accomplishments. However, it has not come without a great price tag. I guess anything worth having in life comes with such a price. Most people would never know what it means to grow up as a preacher's son. They never get to see the stories that unveil themselves within the confines of the church and in the home of a pastor. I have invited you all into the world of "preachers."

My father's name was Jackson Hammond. He was a proud man that had no intention of becoming a pastor, simply being a church member was a stretch for him. It all began in 1975. I was four years old at that time. My father was an up and coming bicycle salesman for an Italian bicycle company in Houston, Texas. He was known for throwing elaborate parties that would last throughout the night into the early morning. My mother Dorothy was a housewife who loved her husband beyond belief. So much so, she stayed at home and raised five boys while my father traveled the country selling bicycle parts. My brothers (Mason, Jordan, Tedmond and Deidrick) and I were like two sets of kids because of the four year gap between Tedmond and myself (Jackson Jr.). They were there for the down years that my parents experienced. Years that no one ever mentions, until now. Those stories are for another day.

They bought a small home in the middle class section of Houston called Scenic Woods. They were destined to find comfort in a quiet neighborhood that would be different than the hard street life they both struggled to get away from. It was odd that this new found peace would drive my mother to find some type of discard to break the silence of middle class America. She soon grew argumentative with my dad whenever he was home. The walls were so paper-thin in our quaint home that you could hear them arguing until the wee hours of the morning. This new life was hard on the both of them and so the next viable thing to do was to find a church. This is where our lives began to change.

One Sunday morning without warning, all five of us were gathered into the station wagon and whisked away to church. I still remember the big sign with letters that read, "Greater Wayside Baptist Church." The music was wonderful and soulful as I had never heard such glorious voices in my short life. Rev. Randy Phillips was the pastor there. He had smooth dark skin, a long-muscular frame and a very long Jeri-curl. If you want a clear and accurate visual, just picture the preacher Arsenio Hall played in Coming to America. Sometimes I wonder if Phillips was his muse for the movie. He preached and spoke of Jesus as if he and Jesus were best friends. His long, flowing black robe was drenched in sweat as he belted out the best homiletics this side of Heaven. Next, his daughter Caroline sang a song that brought the whole church to tears. I sometimes hear her song in my sleep. Apparently, this combination of events led my father to give his hand to the preacher and his heart to Jesus. In other words, we all joined church that day and were better for it.

After a short while, the arguments between my father and mother began to come to a screeching halt. The parties that they were known for stopped completely. There was something different about their relationship that was brand new. And a sure sign that things were different was the day my father took his trademark Marlboro cigarettes and threw them in the trash can. We would never see him pick them up again. The next Sunday my father confessed before the church that the Lord had called him to preach the gospel of Jesus Christ. Our lives once again would see a drastic change for the better.

My father began to talk and act like a Baptist preacher. He would come home from work and pick up his bible and begin reading it. He would read for hours as if he was searching for something within the pages. He no longer had interest in taking me too little league practice because he was always at church. He had church members over to the house and they would have bible study twice a week. He was fully engulfed in his newfound salvation. My mother's transformation was a bit slower but soon she stopped cursing and wearing pants. She was now a preacher's wife and things would have to be different with her. My mother's salvation came at a much slower pace as did my father's. She has always been a staunchly strong woman. I am very much like her in that way. My father always said I should have been named Dorothy Jr. Still not sure if that was a compliment or a put down.

Anyways, my father was now a disciple of Rev.Phillips he was never prouder of anything in his entire life. He was faithful to every church meeting and service. My mother joined the choir and we became a devout church family. The next Sunday was the first time I heard my mother sing. It was as if I was seeing her for the first time. As she sang, she cried and moaned and the congregation loved it. I could see the pride in my father's face as it was his first sermon that Sunday as well. He preached and instantly it was plain to see that he meant every word that he said. In no time at all he became Rev. Phillips right hand man.

Rev. Phillips was an elite minister on the northeast side of Houston. He was then President of the Baptist Preachers Coalition. His wife Sherry was the church pianist and his family all sang in the choir. Caroline, Douglas, and John were his children and they were all close in age to me and my brothers. This made going to church so often a lot more tolerable. There was also the added bonus of three of my older brothers all having crushes on the beautiful Caroline. The church quickly began to grow in numbers from 100 members to about 400 or so believers. With such a growing number of new families, Rev. Phillips named my father Youth Minister and then Assistant Pastor. It was this new appointment that began a curious series of events.

Soon my father began to spend more and more time with Rev. Phillips. They began to develop an inseparable friendship as he was becoming my father's spiritual mentor. My father was learning a lot about being a good minister and about teaching others about the bible. However, one night something peculiar happened after church. As we were waiting on the back pew of the sanctuary, a man walked in the church visibly upset. He said at the top of his voice, "Where the fuck is that jack-legged preacher?" Whelp, that's what he said. I saw my father emerge from the pastor's study in a huff. As the man approached, my father grabbed his arm and began to lead the man outside of the church. We were all scared including my mother because we had no idea what was going to happen to my father.

After a few minutes, my father beckoned for us to get in the car and we drove away. My mother whispered to my father, "What's going on Jackson?" and he replied,

"I'll tell you when we get home." Remember, our walls at home were paper-thin so I heard the whole story. The man was Bob Johnson and he was accusing Rev. Phillips of sleeping with his wife. My father guaranteed the man he must be making some kind of mistake. He also told him that he would talk to Rev. Phillips and clear things up. But when my father asked Rev. Phillips about the affair, he fessed up to the whole thing. That night was the first of only a handful of times that I ever heard my father cry.

My father didn't have many rules but I knew cheating on your wife was probably one rule he adhered too. However, he was willing to forgive Rev. Phillips and did everything he could to keep this away from the congregation. This also included him keeping the truth away from Bob Johnson. I would like to tell you that this was the first and last time that type of situation happened but I would be lying to you. This was not only happening at our church, a few months later it happened at BPC Convocation.

Convocation was an important gathering for the Baptist Preachers Coalition. It was when all of the churches in Texas that were affiliated with the Coalition would converge on Houston or some other designated city. There were twenty five churches that got together and held classes, musicals and services to help keep the Coalition going. However, to my brothers and me, it only meant three days of non-stop church. This year's Convocation would be our first and our last.

The opening night musical was when I first heard the word "homosexual" used in a sentence. My oldest brother Mason used the word to describe the tall, slender man with long hair and fingernails that played the organ. His name was B. Arthur Rhodes and he called everyone Mister or Misses. He called my mother Misses Dorothy Diva because she was fabulous every time he saw her. He wore a red tuxedo trimmed in black with a black cape that he flung back and forth as he played. But the real treat for the kids were the glittery red mules that he wore to compliment his outfit. But as amazing as B. Arthur played the organ he sang just as soulfully. His voice sounded like he was like Prince and Michael Jackson's love child.

However, no great organist is complete without a sidekick. B. Arthur's sidekick was Jimmy "Jacque" Johnson. Jimmy was famous throughout the South for many reasons but none more important to convocation than his choir directing theatrics. This night's performance would include Jimmy doing the split from left to right in the middle of a song. Both Jimmy and B. Arthur were wholly important to convocation because they drew a crowd, "The gay church crowd." The choir was mostly filled with dedicated women that loved to sing and gay men that loved Jimmy and B. Arthur. The duo had a following that would pack the church to the rafters just to catch a glimpse of their act. Of course, all of this information was all new to my father and my family.

After the musical, my younger brother Deidrick (we called him DJ) and I began to sing the songs that the choirs had sang that night in the car. We also entertained my other brothers with imitations of B. Arthur's cape flinging. This did not go over well with my father. Then, my father tried to explain (unsuccessfully) what we had seen that night and why we shouldn't make fun of it all. After a few minutes of uncomfortable silence and glances at us in his rear view mirror, we just shut up. For the life of me I couldn't understand why he was angry about us singing!

The next morning we got dressed and went to the church for classes that lasted all day. But Caroline, Douglas and John Phillips were there and that made the day better for us. We all said our goodbyes that evening and went home to get dressed for the big service that night. My father was so excited he bought a new suit from what we referred to as "The Preacher Shop. "The store was actually called, Mike's Suitors. This is where all the preachers from around the state would come to get tailored suits, shirts and alligator shoes. Rev. Phillips once told another pastor that, "You're not a preacher until you got a pair of gators." So, my dad went into Mike's and got his new tailored suit, a very expensive shirt and his first pair of gators. When we all got home and got dressed my father was the last one to emerge from his bedroom. My mother was waiting for him to come into the living room and reveal his new suit.

Man, I have never seen my father so sharp before in all my days. He looked like Rev. Phillips but with my dad's skin on. He was all smiles as we drove up to the church's packed parking lot. The other pastors were standing in front of the church on display as we got out of our wood-paneled station wagon. As my father emerged, the pastors began to compliment him on his "preacher's garbs." And just like that, they all disappeared into the crowd. We were seated in the preacher's wives section or as it is more commonly known, "Church VIP."

After, the deacons ended devotion we all got a shock when my father was chosen to do the opening prayer. His prayer was so sincere and heartfelt, the church exploded with praises of "Thank you Jesus and Hallelujahs." That prayer would serve to be his coming out party. But he was only the appetizer for that night's service. The main course was a sermon delivered by the notorious Rev. Barry Fowler. Fowler was B. Arthur's first cousin (and traveling musician) and they would travel the South preaching at every church they could find. He was a chiseled, handsome man that stood six foot three and about two hundred and twenty pounds. The ladies all loved him and we would soon find out, so did the men. There was only one problem with that, he was married with two kids.

That night Rev. Fowler prayed (to upstage my father's prayer) for twenty minutes, sang for an hour and preached for another hour. What made this such a spectacular feat was he was drunk as a skunk. The crowd was electric and people were fainting, shouting and running around the church. It was very much like the movie, "The Blues Brothers" in that sense. At one point, he laid down on the floor while he was preaching sending every beautiful woman in the church into a heated frenzy. All of the other pastors were up cheering him on as if they were rooting for their favorite football team. The best was yet to come though. After church, it was customary for all of the pastors to visit the local Lenny's (a popular food spot) along with the musicians. They would use the location to split the money they collected that night. My father was asked by Rev. Fowler himself to be there. So, my mother drove us all home and my father was to ride to Lenny's with Rev. Phillips.

My mother was so proud of my father that night. He was meeting all the men that he looked up to and they were asking him to be a part of the in-crowd. However, something went horribly wrong that night. About three in the morning the house phone rang. It was my father on the other end of the line. It was a short conversation and the next sound I heard was the old station wagon starting. Of course, I stayed up to hear what my father and mother were talking about when they returned. They rushed quickly to their bedroom and closed the door.

They tried to whisper but with paper thin walls that was always impossible. My father told my mother that Rev. Fowler wanted him and the rest of the pastors to visit a strip club. And that's not all; Fowler was seen in the parking lot of Lenny's embracing a man very intimately. That's when my father made up an excuse about a sick kid and called my mother to come and pick him up. Both my parents seemed to be heartbroken that night.

The very next morning was the family and friends service at our church. I heard my father tell my mother that night that he was going to find another church for us. My father sat there in church with tears in his eyes and was visibly bothered by the presence of the men he knew were imposters. After the service was over we sat in our usual back pew waiting for my father to emerge from the Pastor's study. There was another person in our party that Sunday and she was whispering something to my mother. I could see my father walking towards us appearing to be very sad and Rev. Phillips was calling his name to come back. That's when the lady that was talking to my mother stood up and introduced herself.

Her name was Rose Moreland. Miss Rose was an older fifty-something year old woman that looked like she was classy. She wore an all-black suit, white gloves and a fancy hat. She asked, "Are you Rev. Hammond?" And my father replied, "Yes, I am, how do you do?" Mrs. Rose told my father that one of the Deacons from her church heard him pray at Convocation and thought he would be a good fit to pastor their church. My mother looked at my father and they both smiled in delight. We, on the other hand were completely upset about the thought of having to leave Greater Wayside.

After talking to Miss Rose for about thirty minutes my father and mother got into the car where we were all waiting for them. We all were hoping that this was some kind of sick joke. When my father got in the car, he dropped the bad news on us. He told us that we would be visiting First Heights Baptist Church on next Sunday to preach and if everything went well he would be the pastor of that church. My parents were happy but we were all very sad. Even mom's pork chops that Sunday couldn't fix us being separated from sweet singing Caroline and our other friends. This would be the longest week ever.

The next Sunday came and we were all dragging around the house. None of us were at the table for my father's traditional Sunday morning pancakes. My mother had to come into our rooms and make us come to the table. Breakfast was quiet and boring until I finally let the air out of the room. I asked my father, "Do we really have to go to this dumb church?" My father simply replied, "Yes, and it's not a dumb church." Then, DJ chimed in with, "It is so dumb. "That's when my mother's Christianity regressed a bit as she began whooping my little brother across the head with a banana. Little chunks of banana were flying all over the place. And then there was a great silence! No one wanted any part of that banana. In the quiet, I could not help thinking about how hurt Rev. Phillips appeared to be when my father left. The strip club, the affairs and the homosexuality of preachers was all so confusing to me. I was going to miss that church but mostly, I would miss the candy store that was directly across the street.

CHAPTER 2:
THE GREAT AWAKENING

After we all beheld the wrath of my mother we gathered our bibles and headed to what would become our new church home. After driving for at least an hour, we couldn't find the place! The way Rose Moreland spoke and dressed, it gave us the indication we were looking for a grand cathedral. We drove for another half hour in that old wood paneled station wagon looking for First Heights Baptist Church. In frustration to my dad, (but in delight to us) he had almost given up. But alas, he went to the gas station to use the pay phone and called Mrs. Rose. We all hoped and prayed she didn't answer but she did. My father climbed back into the car and said, "You remember that little white house we kept passing? Well, that's the church. "My mother replied, "That's the church?" We all said in unison, "That's the church?"

My father drove about five miles per hour back to that little white house. It seemed like an eternity getting there again. When we pulled up Mrs. Rose (who had the same outfit on as she did when we met her) was waiting on the curb. Also, the lone deacon of the church was there to greet us as well. His name was Emmitt Dockers. He stood about four foot nine inches tall; he wore a paper bag brown suit with a hat that looked as old as he was. He looked crazy as hell. We could only imagine what the inside of the church actually looked like. As we entered the house (church), there were six benches on each side, a beat up piano, and a pastor's study with the only bathroom in the church. The pulpit was a make shift wood podium that also served as the choir stand. To us, it was our worst nightmares come true. To my father, it was Heaven. I thought he would rush us all into the wagon and head back to our old church and beg Rev. Phillips for forgiveness. However, that was not the case.

I knew we were staying when the title of my father's message was, "I will not back down from the Devil. "He preached like someone was holding his family hostage and he had to preach for our release. Mrs. Rose and Deacon Dockers stood up, cheered and my mother cried. The other four church members that were there did the same. That's right, there were only four other people there besides our family, Mrs. Rose and Deacon Dockers. But my father didn't seem to care. He hooped and hollered for what seemed like an eternity. It was so hot in the building his new suit was drenched with sweat like he had just played basketball in the evening sun. He must have made an impression because when he got back in the car he told my mother the good news. He was now the proud pastor of First Heights Baptist Church. He also said next Sunday we would all have to join this new church (house).

My mother wasn't so convinced about this new endeavor. She smiled and kissed my dad but I could see the old Dorothy coming out of her. She gave us this look like is this man crazy? Does he see what we see? But nonetheless, she spent the entire week inviting all of our friends and family to the new church (house). My father spent the week looking for supplies to fix the benches. My mother had ruined her good dress when she sat on a rusty nail on one of the cheaply built benches. He had called some of his cousins to help him fix up the church. They also bought microphones, speakers and even fixed the piano that was broken. This only meant one thing to us; we weren't going back to Greater Wayside.

The next Sunday, we all joined church. I cried the whole time and everyone thought I was feeling the spirit. I wasn't, I was feeling like this is a huge mistake. There were more people there that Sunday too. Mrs. Rose's family all came and they joined church as well. Now there were 18 members of the church. And by the next two months, there were 100 members of the church. Word was spreading like wildfire concerning the handsome young pastor that could preach like nobody's business. By that time, my family wasn't the only members of the choir. There was no music in the church and I couldn't stand it. My father couldn't stand it either. One Saturday I answered the phone at home and a familiar voice came on the line asking for my father. My father seemed surprised to be hearing from the caller.

After he got off the phone he called out to my mother. When she walked into the room he laid the good news on her. Both B. Arthur Rhodes and Jimmy Jack Johnson wanted to come our church. I was so confused about the whole thing. Didn't he just want to slap us silly for imitating these guys?

Why would he want them to come to our church? But, come Sunday morning they were both there. B. Arthur was his usual flashy self with his green leisure suit and green cape with matching mules. He model-walked into the small church and greeted my mother with, "well we meet again Misses Dorothy Diva." Jimmy Jack had his usual tuxedo shirt with a black bell bottom suit. They sang and entertained for two hours that morning and 10 people joined the church. It was looking like this was a match made in Heaven.

After church my father invited B. Arthur and Jimmy Jack to have lunch with us at "Fish Kitchen. "During lunch I kept staring at B. Arthur's pressed hair. I stared so much while no was looking he leaned over the table and said, "Boo. "He scared the Be 'Jesus out of me! But while I was staring I noticed that B. Arthur and Jimmy both wore matching rings. They behaved like an old married couple. They were completing each other sentences and going on about preachers and choirs. Even at that age, I knew something was different about them. I just couldn't put my finger on it. They promised my father that they would be dedicated and build the best choir Houston has ever seen. And that is exactly what they did. People came from everywhere to that small church. In less than a year we had over 400 members and had outgrown the church. My father decided it was time to build a new church.

That was not the only big decision he would make either. He also decided to leave his big paying job and pastor a church full time. Our lives would never be the same again! We needed someplace to hold church services while our new building was going up. We moved in with a pastor two blocks over mainly because he needed the money and we had very little to spend. It worked out for the both of us. This preacher's name was Devin Beatty. Pastor Beatty was older and some would say a little senile. However, he was a good man. His sermons were never longer than ten minutes. And he had maybe ten members in his church that didn't share his last name. But at least he had a choir stand and a working organ. He also had a single deacon that was his right hand man. Deacon Lett was only matched in zaniness by our own Deacon Dockers. These two were kindred spirits. During devotion, they would have "who can pray the longest contests" and held up church with such long elaborate battle-prayers.

They were good men though and were highly devoted to their pastors. They were so devoted that one night they almost put an angel out of service. That faithful night the neighborhood wine-o wandered into our church looking for money. You could smell the Old English 800 from the choir stand he was so loaded. Deacon Lett and Dockers ran to the back to ask the man to leave but my father wouldn't let them. He said, "Mister I want to pray for you." The two deacons brought the man to the front of the church and my father began to pray for him. At that point, something mysterious happened. The man began to sober up. His eyes rolled in the back of his head and he began talking like he had sense. He told my father his name was Leo Gold. And God told him to tell my father that he was going to build a great church and he was going to be a Holy Ghost preacher. This was strange considering no one told Leo we were building a church. The ink was barely dry on the plans my father had drawn up.

He also told my father to go to a car dealership and tell

them to give him a car and raffle it off and that's how they would pay for the church. Needless to say, everyone including my father was speechless. Then Leo Gold turned and walked out of the church never to be seen again. My father drove us around the Heights looking for Leo all night after church. We couldn't find a trace of him. The next day, my father drove to a local car dealership and asked the man for a car that the church could raffle off. And Holy Toledo, it happened just as the wine-o said it would. The man at the dealership even agreed to let my father put it on a trailer and show it off at the local mall. We raised $60,000 on a single car. It was three times what the car was worth. It was more than enough to pay off everyone who would build the church. That was the easy part of the Old English 800 prophesy. Neither my father nor any of us had ever heard the term, "Holy Ghost preacher." Did he mean my dad would die and come back as some kind of ghost preacher? I could tell that notification baffled my father as well.

Six months later we marched two blocks from the old

church into the new one building. It was the grandest church I had ever seen. It even had air conditioning. The best part of the new building was no one could hear you flush the toilet while service was going on like in the old church. Our choir now had robes to sing in. They were B. Arthur originals with bright red outlines and fancy initials running down the front shingles or whatever you call those things that hang off the front of robes. He even had us doing a two-step down the aisle as we walked to the choir stand. I think Mrs. Rose even fainted a few times that Sunday. And to top all of that, Rev. Phillips and Greater Wayside would be there to Christian the new church. The entire group of preachers from the Baptist Preachers Coalition would also be there that day. It seemed that they had apologized to my father for their indiscretions and wanted to make him apart of their Coalition again. It was also a fact that a new church this size would mean more money coming into the BPC as well.

All was right with the world now that we got to see

our old church family and the fancy preachers of BPC. It was like we never left Greater Wayside. That was until Rev. Fowler walked in and saw B. Arthur and Jimmy Jack were members of my father's church. After church, there was some commotion going on outside in the parking lot. Jimmy Jack and Rev. Fowler were exchanging expletives with each other. It appeared that B. Arthur and Rev. Fowler weren't cousins after all. They were more like kissing cousins. That's why B. Arthur was no longer playing the organ for Rev. Fowler. Deacon Dockers stepped in and told the men it wasn't Christ-like to be cussing on church grounds. That's when Rev. Fowler unleashed a might profanity laced tirade upon (including the word "Fuck") Deacon Dockers. Whelp, that's what he said. Oh no! They were ruining our great awakening. Deacon Dockers held his tongue and made the men get into their cars and leave. My father never heard of this incident because it would have broken his heart. He never realized that B. Arthur and Jimmy Jack were lovers. We were all gullible back then and believed Jesus could heal anybody. He fully believed these men were just fighting as hard as they could to not be the way that they were.

Jimmy Jack would even bring women to choir rehearsal with him to help the choir. When my father would come out of his office Jimmy Jack would pretend to be romantically interested in the woman. My mother knew he was only pretending along with everyone else in the choir. No straight man would wear Gloria Vanderbilt jeans and ankle boots to church. However, we loved them all the same because when it came down to it, they were good people.

That perception would change a few months later. There was a rumor that B. Arthur and Rev. Fowler mending their fences and he even left his wife for him. Jimmy Jack was heartbroken. He wasn't the same old firecracker choir director he used to be. It was hard for him to pretend that B. Arthur hadn't broken his heart. Jimmy Jack had decided to move closer to the church into his own house. So, he asked one of the scrapping young men at the church to help him paint his house. When we heard Jimmy Jack was offering fried chicken for helping him, all five of us volunteered as well. We spent the whole day at his house painting and scraping every inch of his house. My mother came and picked us up at five o'clock leaving Jimmy Jack and the young man there alone. Later that night, my father received a phone call from the young man's father saying that Jimmy Jack tried to get his son's booty. Whelp, that's what he said. We wouldn't see Jimmy Jack or B. Arthur for a long time after that phone call.

You would think such a frightening event would be the off limits to any of us but it wasn't. We were kids after all. Whenever one of us would get out of line my older brother would say, "Hey, you better straighten up or I'll call Jimmy Jack to get your booty. "Kids can be so cruel. We never let our parents know that we knew what happened that day. We just thought we were painting someone's house that was a cool, quirky guy. Jimmy Jack was lost and I felt sorry for him but also ashamed of him at the same time. But most importantly, I always wondered if he was alright. I thought, losing your best friend must be really, really hard, especially for Jimmy Jack. I know for sure it was very hard on the choir to lose such animated, hard-working and caring people like those two were. I guess all good things come to an end. This was one of the saddest events that transpired at our church. But no one would dare address the issue out loud. What is a preacher without an organ and a hell of a choir director?

Chapter 3:

Preacher Kindergarten

My father became an avid student of the Bible. He was a teaching preacher. He had even graduated to teaching the rest of the preachers on fourth Sunday evenings at the BPC's monthly service. Things were moving very fast for him in ministry. It was moving even faster for him in aggravation with the other preachers. They were all good men but their lifestyles were so different than what his was. For instance, there were the money men, Rev. Bobby Bones and Rev. Fred Flowers. They would beg for money during the offering period like they were auctioning salvation. Then there were the slobs like Rev. Little and Rev. Brown who each had children outside of their marriage. What is worse was that their baby's mothers were still members of their church. But that's a different book for another time.

The next group was Rev. Fowler and his gang of down-low brothers. The end of the 80's would bring an end to their passiveness in declaring their affection for men. It soon became apparent that these men no longer caved to public perception and did little to hide their sexual preference. They would later become known as the "Family." I must say they paled in comparison to the outright whores like Rev. Phillips, Rev. Davis and Rev. Mores. These doppelgangers ran rampant through the women in BPC faster than the Bird flu through China. But they all looked like a million bucks, drove fancy cars and wore the best suits church money could buy. It was quickly becoming a circus in BPC. Finally, my father had enough and quit once again. The only thing worse than being a part of BPC, is quitting BPC. They ran my father's name through the mud every chance they could. He became known as "Holier than thou."

This bad blood and feud took its toll on my father. We

knew he missed the prestige and power of BPC but he couldn't just sit there and fester in their hog- wash they were selling. I thought he may change his mind but the next Sunday he denounced BPC and refused to acknowledge Rev. Phillips as his pastor. As a result, we had most of the pretty women in our church leave. And, most of the men who had joined because of B. Arthur and Jimmy Jack had already left as well. The church was now floating aimlessly without clear direction during this time.

One night my father was invited to his classmate's church to hear him preach. The man's name was Shawn Lemon. Elder Lemon was an old throwback preacher. He wore suits from the 70's, his hair was slicked back and he always wore white shoes. He called them his preaching shoes. It was at that service my father finally found out what a Holy Ghost preacher was. After hearing Elder Lemon speak, my father was convinced he no longer wanted to be associated with the Baptist Church. He was now a Holiness preacher. Say what? I said, he said, he was now a Holiness preacher. That night he received the baptism of the Holy Ghost with evidence of speaking in tongues. Say what? Never mind. He was on a different path now to the kingdom of God. Next Sunday he would lay the news on the whole church.

If you know anything about the Baptist church, back then they did not care to discuss the Holy Ghost. They just want to go to church, sing, flirt a little, hear the word and go home. So, when my father dropped the bomb on over 400 Baptist church members that Sunday, you could hear a pin drop. I distinctly remember all the curls falling out of Mrs. Rose hair simultaneously. My father had to take the whole church to preacher kindergarten to fully explain the new direction of the church. After church, there was an emergency meeting called by Mrs. Rose and the deacons. She wanted my father's head on a platter. He must be loony tunes to think they were going to support him on this one. However, the deacons sided with my father and Mrs. Rose left with half of the church. My father had made a stand, but at what cost?

My father remained unfazed by the walkout. The next week Elder Lemon preached a revival at our church. That man preached for several hours non-stop and his mouth would become parched and white stuff would form in the corners of his mouth. My brothers and I would tell people when they had white stuff in the corners of their mouth that they had some Elder Lemon on their mouth. He was very hard to understand because all of this Holiness stuff was still brand new to us. My father wondered why we hadn't caught the Holy Ghost yet. So, the last night of the revival I faked it to shut him up. The rest of my brothers followed suit and did the same thing. We would later laugh at ourselves when we got home.

Our church was officially "baptized in the Holy Ghost" during that long, long week of revival. It didn't take long to see that the traditional two hour church service was now a thing of the past. This is the best way I can sum up a holiness church service. First, these people don't show up for church until 8:30 at night. Next, you start with a testimony service. This is when every crazy person in the congregation has a chance to stand up and testify about the goodness of the Lord. Some people go on and on for what seems like hours pointing out every illness known to man that God has delivered them from. They testify about their children, their unsaved husbands, friends and their bosses. Some saints even sing songs to go along with their testimony. If you think the testimony can go on for hours, the songs go on even longer. Then they play the "shouting music" which takes another hour before it's done.

Now it's ten o'clock, and this is when the praise and worship begins. This is easily an hour long process because of all the songs. Then, by eleven the preacher finally gets up and does his thing. His thing depends on which preacher is preaching. If he is a "rah-rah" preacher he is going to read a few scriptures and then get down to the whooping and hollering. If he is a teaching preacher he is going to put you to sleep after fifteen minutes but he will still preach for at least an hour and a half. If he is a prophetic preacher, you may have to drink a cup of coffee because you are going to be there all night. These types of preachers won't stop until they have laid hands on everyone in the church. Lastly, it will be offering time. Offering time ranges from forty five minutes to an hour. The preacher begins with asking for $1000 and works his way down to a $3 offering. The $3 dollar offering is known as the "Trinity "offering. This is the famous "don't feel bad cause you don't have a $1000 offering" but the preacher makes you feel bad cause you don't give the $1000 offering. I say that because the people giving the $1000 get the good prophecies like healings, cars, houses and new jobs. The trinity offering people get a "God bless you" from the preacher. This whole process can make for a very, very long night for those who are brave enough to endure such church services.

The last type of preacher is the most sought after in the Holiness church. They have rock band followers that travel all over the city to hear them preach. They are the "Healing and Deliverance" preachers. The most famous preacher we ever encountered was Bishop Thomas Bethune or as he was better known as "the man with oil in his hand. "Bethune was a very arrogant man. He had long, gray, curly hair that made him resemble a somewhat taller and darker George Washington. He was always late and held the congregation hostage for hours during offering time. But his big act was praying for the sick and casting demons out of people. For a cool $1000 he would pray for you and forecast sunny skies and green pastures. But first, he would tell you, "There are some things inside of you that the Lord says must come out." And that's when he says the anointing oil would flow out his deformed hand. He said he was born with this deformity and when the anointing comes that holy oil would flow out of his deformed hand. The people would come from miles to see this great wonder. He just seemed like a creepy old guy to me.

He once laid hands on me and it burned like fire. I was blown away because I actually felt something special happened to me at church. They took Bishop Bethune to lunch the last day of the revival. Before the revival started my father received a phone call in his study from the couple. It seemed that the Bishop's hand may have been deformed but his sex drive was perfectly normal. The married couple told my father Bishop Bethune offered them $4000 to have a threesome with them. My father ended up preaching the last night of the revival himself. It was like déjà vu all over again for my father.

Over the years we would learn about all kinds of preacher tricks and gimmicks. Don't get me wrong, there were some very real preachers that were gifted and anointed. One of the most prolific prophets that ever walked the face of the Earth was Willy Flanders. If he told you the moon was made out of cheese, you better go buy crackers. There were no tricks, no gimmicks just pure prophecy. One night there was a small boy who had not spoken in four years since his father passed. The boy's mother had been to every revival known to man trying to get her soon healed. Prophet Flanders called the boy to the alter and laid hands on him and told his mother that her son would speak by the next morning. He also told her she was going to come into a large sum of money in the next few days. The next day, the woman brought her son by the church and he was speaking for the first time in four years. By that Wednesday, the woman decided to play the lottery and ended up winning $1.2 million dollars. The woman promised to pay her tithes to Prophet Flanders church and give him a love offering. However, the woman and her son were never seen again.

These were only a few of the events that would take place in our church now. We were becoming a nesting ground for great revivals and great change. People's lives were changing and so were our lives. The church was growing by leaps and bounds and the entire city seemed to be moving in the direction of holiness. Yes there were some bad apples and crazy people along the way but for the most part it was a wonderful experience. It was absolutely necessary for us to experience the bad apples because it showed us how to deal with these types of preachers. Some were there to help my father and some were there to rip his congregation to shreds by taking their offerings and church members with them. It was not uncommon for a preacher to walk in for a three day revival and take a portion of your church with them as they left. These basic laws of Holiness taught our young church many, many hard lessons.

PREACHERS

CHAPTER 4:

CRUSADE 87

The year is now 1987, the best year our church would ever have financially and spiritually. Having been duped and disappointed so far in his formative years of preaching my father had an idea. He wanted to hear from God. He had a well-thought out vision. He would have a revival. Not just any revival but, seven consecutive weeks of revival. He would call it Crusade 87. There were t-shirts, bumper stickers and hats all promoting this mighty move of God that I called Crusade Insanity. This was unprecedented and unheard of in our city for a church to hold service seven days a week for seven consecutive weeks. Nevertheless, when my father makes a declaration over the pulpit it's a done deal. These crusades were all about my father wanting to clean up the Holiness church and purge his members from the drudges of church society.

The first week was my favorite week of the entire crusade. It was kicked off by Bishop Bowden. He had an enormous church nearby and he was prime time. We visited his church once and I was immediately impressed. Not only did he have the best choir and singers but when he got up to preach the lights went off. When the lights came back on he had theme music. The church sang in unison, "The Stone of Salvation", which was the church anthem. It was like being at an Earth, Wind and Fire concert. "Bishop Bowden was a middle-aged, handsome and had enough "bling" to blind you. He flashed a gold nugget watch, rings on most of his fingers and a golden cross. He was the ultimate preacher. Bishop Bowden preached the entire week until his voice was hoarse. People were falling out all over the place and the music played all night long. Heck, we almost ran out of shouting blankets. You know the ones the ushers use to cover up people when they pass out from shouting? It was that Friday night that I met a woman that would a big part of my life. Her name was Mother Anderson. When a woman has shown wisdom and has been a positive role model in the church she is deemed a "Mother." Mother Anderson was much like Mrs. Rose. She was fancy and dignified. And when she talked, everyone listened to her aged and raspy wisdom. She walked up to me and said, "You not fooling me young man, you're going to be a great Man of God and a great man." This was probably the only time in my life I remained speechless. It was like her words were true and they cut right through me. She also scared me half to death with her cold-dark preachy eyes.

When that first week was over I thought I'd never see her again. But on Sunday morning there she was with her preachy eyes again. The next move would shock everyone at church. She joined our church. Why? Why would she leave the Stone of Salvation? Her preacher was like an icon? She told us that Sunday that God told her our church needed her more. I know I was happy but Bishop Bowden wasn't so happy. However, my father immediately called Bishop Bowden after church to tell him the news. To our surprise he was not upset about Mother Anderson's defection. As a show of good faith Bishop Bowden would return for the next two weeks of the crusade. He was now my father's new mentor.

The second week of the crusade was conducted by Prophet Flanders. He was averaging ten new members and nearly $10,000 dollars a night. He was also averaging about four hours of preaching and prophecy a night. That Thursday night the funniest and most bizarre thing happened. His organist began plunking around on the organ uncontrollably while Flanders was preaching. Flanders stopped preaching and told the man to "come down off that organ." The man shook his head, no. The church erupted in laughter as Flanders began chasing the man around the church. It was hilarious. Finally, Flanders slipped and fell and twisted his ankle but as the portly preacher was falling to the ground his pants fell down around his ankles. One of the ushers quickly threw a shouting blanket over him but the damage had already been done. This would be the only night the crusade ended before 1 a.m.

The third week was conducted by my father's soon to be best friend. Rev. Kevin Dollar. He too was a converted Baptist preacher. My father had preached for him a few years ago when Dollar was trying to get his church started. The Sunday my father preached for him he gave Rev. Dollar an envelope and told him not to open it until he left. The enveloped contained a crisp one hundred dollar bill. My father never realized that one hundred dollar bill he gave Dollars' church was the exact amount of money they needed to finish their new building. It was a sentiment that Dollar would never forget. He presented my father with a one hundred dollar bill plaque in remembrance of what he had done.

Money was important to this man for a variety of reasons. He was moved by a televangelist preaching about wealth, faith and prosperity of believers. Dollar told a story about him and wife being on welfare and food stamps. He said he was preaching to people about the goodness of God and here he was buying food for his family with food stamps. At that moment, he decided to believe God for his needs and would never use food stamps again. He taught himself how to manage money and taught his members how to take care of the Man of God. It was something new about giving and tithing that we had never heard before. Baptist preachers never spend more than five minutes teaching about money. They spend hours asking for money but not teaching about it. It was just implied that the church was going to give it up and that's that.

Dollar spent the majority of the night explaining about giving and the faith it takes to give when you don't have it. We had no idea that this new age teachings would spread like wildfire all across the country and would usher in the 90's in grand fashion. He was a visionary. Unlike the other Holiness preachers who had preached before him Dollar was done by 11 pm. However, my father would get up, talk and lay hands on people until

1:30 a.m. He was trying out his new preaching style on the unsuspecting congregation. It is now the end of week three and we are exhausted.

Just when everyone thought this was getting to be a bad idea, Abby Anderson came to town. Yes Abby! A woman preacher was preaching in our church. She also happened to be the daughter of Mother Anderson. Abby was a gargantuan, plus sized women with a short Jeri-curl and horned-rim glasses. And when she opened her mouth it was like an earthquake happened. Her sermon on her first night blew the church away. How could this be happening? A Baptist preacher would never let a woman preach in their pulpit. But we were no longer Baptist and Abby was rolling. She came complete with her own entourage and media ministry. She was selling cassette tapes of her sermons like hot cakes. With her love offerings and tape sells she easily walked away with $20, 000 dollars for the week. It was nothing we had ever seen before. She out-preached, out sang and raised more money than any of the other preachers before or after her.

There was a question about whether Abby liked men
or women though. Unlike many other preachers all
you had to do was hang out with them after church and
you would know. She had Mother Anderson's since of
refinement in that regard and was very discrete about
her preference. I don't think anyone will ever know
or ask that question. A few years later, we heard from
Mother Anderson that Abby was in town. My father
and I went to see her preach. It was a church on the
other side of town. She did her thing once again and we
enjoyed it richly. After church we were waiting to talk
to her after everyone had left. Suddenly, there was a big
thump coming from the pastor's study. We ran to see
what had happened. Abby was upset about receiving a
check for preaching when she asked for cash. Much like
rock stars everyone knows you do not give a preacher a
check for preaching. It is a cash and carry business. With
one punch Abby had knocked the male pastor out cold.
As we helped the man to his feet he told his deacons to

give Abby the cash she asked for. She apologized to the man and my father for having to see her act like that. My father whispered to me, "don't tell your mother", I promised him I wouldn't, until now. I would have to keep a lot of secrets from both my mother and father in the coming years but it was fine with me. I knew all the gossip that my brothers didn't know, until now.

The next week Elder Colonel Thompson came to town. He was the true definition of a smooth operator. He would often pose and smile for the lady folk at church. He would always mention he was married but never had his wife with him. He was a traveling evangelist. During his sermons, he would shout, "Gawd, told me to tell you", and all of the kids would laugh. My brothers and I would imitate him all night long. His sermons were so long we would sneak out of the church and play in the streets and then go back inside and he was still preaching. Every now and then Deacon Franks would come outside and smoke a cigarette. We knew he wouldn't tell because we knew his wife didn't want him smoking. I don't remember much of Elder Thompson but years later he would be one of the most famous televangelist in history with his famous "Gawd, told me to tell you" line.

The sixth week was a country preacher by the name of Brian Brown. He was a Holiness preacher at a Baptist church. Those two don't mix very well if you didn't know. He was a Frenchman with hazel eyes and had really wavy hair, a decent build but he had an enormous ass. Whelp, he did. I know because I overheard my mother tell her cousin on the phone, "Girl, when he holy dance, he makes his booty talk. "I didn't understand what she was talking about until years later. Brown sang and played the organ like he was Stevie Wonder. All the lades lingered after church and rushed over to tell Rev. Brown how much he had touched them by his preaching. I don't think it was his preaching that they wanted to touch. It was his enormous ass. Okayyyy? I don't think it was his preaching that they wanted to touch. It was his enormous ass.

Brown was from my father's hometown and still resided there. His slow southern drawl was evidence that he was not as polished as the other preachers that came before him. His offering skills were not as refined as the other preachers. But because so many women came out to see him he ended up raising about much money as Abby Anderson. There was only one problem with all of this; he didn't like the ladies.

We didn't know this information at the time but it all makes sense now. The preacher that was to conduct the next week's revival was there every night. And when Rev. Brown left, he left with the other preacher. Brown declined all of my father's lunch and dinner invitation which is customary for my father. He also didn't say much in the pastor's study and when he did it was in that soft, gentile southern drawl. Despite all the tomfoolery and shenanigans, souls were being saved, the captives were being set free and the sick were being healed. Wasn't that the purpose of the crusade anyway? The way the preachers behaved was actually the game within the game for me. I was becoming addicted to knowing the sociology of religion that was taking place. Or in other words, I was just plain old nosy.

The final week was strangely awesome. Elder Jake Turnerwall had the honors of closing out this great crusade. This man was Dr. Strange. He always preached in a robe instead of a suit. Traditionally, no one but the pastor of a church wears a robe while preaching at your church. He was quiet for about two minutes and then said, his robe was for protection from evil spirits. Then he shocked the crowd by saying, "There's a witch in this building right now."

I was scared as all get out. And so were the other members of the church. He called this lady out and told her she was a witch and told her to go back to the gates of Hell where she belonged. All of a sudden, the woman began to move around like a snake on the floor. And she had white dust that flew from her purse as she fell. I was thinking, this may be the best show of them all. And it was. It was an ordeal that lasted until four in the morning. Then he called for people to come to the church at noon to pray so the church would be cleansed of the demons that were casts out of the woman. Some people were so scared they didn't come back the next night. If it had not been for him saying he would bless people's wallets and purses on Wednesday night his week would have been a flop. He justified the slow Tuesday night by saying, "People who aren't right with God won't come hear a preacher that can see into their souls." No, you're just plain ole scary Jake Turnerwall.

Friday night he shocked everyone in the building by telling my mother the contents of her purse. He also told her how much money she had down the very penny. I don't know how he knew that information but he did. He told this woman that she had cancer, what kind of cancer and in how many days God was going to heal her. Once again, he was accurate. This mystery man was too much. After Saturday night's service is when I was clued in on his relationship with Brian Brown.

They both finally agreed to have a late night dinner with my parents at the preacher restaurant hang out. After a few minutes, I had to use the bathroom really bad so I excused myself from the table. Remember when I said I never saw B. Arthur for a while? I didn't actually see him but I heard him in the bathroom talking to another organist. I put my feet up on the toilet so they wouldn't know I was there.

B. Arthur was asking the other organist who those preachers were with my father. The organist said they were Brian Brown and Jake Turnerwall. B. Arthur said the one with the big ass is fine but I see he married. The organist said, "That don't mean a damn thang, they lovers boo-boo." The organist said he used to play the organ for Turnerwall and would see them making out late night in the parking lot of the church.

Then the organist asked, "What about that fine red preacher?" B. Arthur told the man that my father was the kindest man he has ever worked for. He also said he's seen a lot of preachers but that Rev. Hammond is a good one and he's for real. Then, they left the bathroom. I was relieved that my father was thought of in a positive light. I was beginning to question how all these janky preachers could pull the wool over my father's eyes. Was he one of them? I knew he wasn't but I wanted to know he wasn't. I felt like a tremendous burden had been lifted off me that night. I would never doubt my father's dedication to doing the right thing again.

On the way home, I told my father what B. Arthur and the organist had said about Brown and Turnerwall. He asked me was I sure? I told him that I was very sure. I even said the big ass part. The next night (the closing night of Crusade 87) my father told the church that the Lord told him to close out the crusade himself. I guess I had been the voice of the Lord to my father that night. It truly was meant for him to preach that night because the church was packed. It was so packed people were standing up and sitting in the choir stand.

You know what happens when the spotlight is on my father? He was "T.D. Jakesulous" that night. He preached like I had never heard him preach before. He was even singing some of the songs we learned from the other churches. He was on a roll. He laid hands on the sick, he prophesied to people and people started running to the front and throwing money in the buckets. There was this crazy dance that he would do when he got "happy." Happy means you are feeling the Holy Spirit and you got dance. His dance kind of reminds me of Elaine Benes trying to dance of Seinfeld. The music was loud and played on and on for hours. Bishop Bowden even joined in on the preaching when my father passed out on the floor. It was like watching a wrestling match. That night I finally felt the feeling that I had been waiting on. I was "catching the Holy Ghost." Maybe it was my pride in seeing my father preach like that or maybe it was a spiritual awakening for me. I just knew something was different this time. It sure wasn't the cinnamon holy oil that's for sure. Crusade 87 went down as the best thing that ever happened to our church and for the city for that matter. We grew by 120 members, our finances were great and we learned a lot about how not to be duped. Whenever there is such a drastic change in a church's environment, the devil gets busy. Boy was he ever!

Our church began to overflow on Sunday mornings. People came from everywhere hoping to get saved, delivered or healed. Some even came looking for love. The pastor from the church a few blocks from us got really upset by our newfound prosperity as well. He put up a billboard that read, "NO GIMMICKS, NO TRICKS, JUST JESUS." This was an obvious slap in the face to my father. However, this did not stop the masses from flocking to the church where God was performing miracles. The next logical growth step for our church was radio and television. Another local up and coming preacher alerted my dad about the attention that radio draws to your church. His name was Tommy Riverdale and he was the proud pastor of the smallish trailer-church called Riverdale Baptist Church. He was a blonde haired, short, fire and brimstone preaching white guy. Whelp, he was! When my father first met him, he was struggling mightily with his ministry. His congregation was only about fifty members strong. His clothes were ratty and his wife, well, she wasn't exactly happy about the church's location. Riverdale was smack-dab in the middle of one of the roughest neighborhoods on the north side of Houston. His members looked more like the cast of the prison show Oz than they did Sunday morning worshippers. Nevertheless, Rev. Tommy was a good man. He preached the walls down every Sunday and took time out to inspire and assist younger preachers like my father. He taught him the radio ministry and how to preach to a radio audience. In no time at all, both ministries were bursting from the seams. They both rather enjoyed the limelight and the new attention that the broadcast was giving them. Riverdale starting receiving a lion's share of the attention (for obvious reasons) and moved from radio to another upstart television company, the Christian Broadcasting Station (CBN). To just about everyone's surprise, Tommy Riverdale was a big-timer in the preaching game but he still remained faithful to the people that helped him. That was until, Tommy built himself a grand-ole church. It was the size of a small city. Remember when I said his wife wasn't too happy about the location of the church? Well, she got her wish. Tommy moved the church to uppity part of town. His grand cathedral was right in the center of Richville, Houston. It was high cotton. Sadly, none of the other preachers did not know how to reach Tommy anymore. So, they were left to fend for themselves in the radio and T.V. game.

And figure it out they did. My father also moved to television as well. Nope, not CBN. It was just your neighborhood friendly community access television station. It wasn't all the bells and whistles CBN had, but it was television. I remember once leading a song with the choir and they put it on the air. They teased me for months about that song. My buddies would see me in the locker room and say, "save me Lord, save me Lord." I took it in stride though because at least my dad was famous for the right reasons. That same broadcast caught the attention of a local gospel singer and his organ-playing wife. Lester and Gena Davis had actual songs on the radio. And Gena had the looks of Beyoncé and the voice of angel. Lester was an exact replica of Billy D. Williams and he knew it. He even tried to talk real slow and pointed like Billy D. They heard my dad preaching on the radio and wanted to join our church. No, they actually said, "The Lord told them to join our church. "What? We already had a musician and I was the lead vocalist at our church. Why are they trying to take my shine? Jesus didn't tell you that woman. But how would my father handle this strange and new problem? Of course, he fired the current musician and hired Lester and Gena. My initial thoughts were that they had something up their sleeves but I couldn't prove it. Later, you will see how right I was about that premonition. For now, Lester was wowing the crowd on Sundays with his silky smooth voice and theatrics. Gena was moving the crowd with her slick organ playing and smoking hot body. We had more men join the church after she arrived than at any other time I can remember. The church couldn't hold all the people that were coming through the doors. Then, the other shoe dropped just like that. Gena wanted to produce a full studio album. Church albums were the latest craze. You want to fill your church up really fast? Put out an album and every hired gun in Houston will be there the next Sunday.

I would like to say the "Save Souls for Christ" album brought hundreds of thousands of new members to our church but I'd be lying. I would only be telling half the story. The album caused more trouble than it was worth. Gena caught Lester cheating with another woman and their marital squabbles carried over into the rehearsals. We also heard Lester had a mean left hook and liked to show it off to his wife. But that's just plain ole gossip. What is true was that all of us usual song leaders were pushed out of the way for ringers. They were Gena and Lester's hired guns and they created a mighty fuss in the choir. By the time the day came to record, a third of the choir was gone. We were starting to lose our way because of this not so dynamic duo. To make matters worse, Lester brought his cousin Albert Johnson to our church. He was the messiest man that ever walked the face of the Earth. Although he was kind, he was still messy. He also thought he was God's gift to women folk. He constantly wore a Crayola-red three piece suit, black shoes with a red heel and also sported a Jeri-curl five years its expiration date. But he was somebody's preacher and howdy. When he sang, women were known to melt like a snow cone in a mid-July heat. His songs felt like cool summer evenings sitting on the porch with mother sipping iced tea. I know it's rather corny but it's true. There is nothing more fantastic than a preacher that can sang. His only flaw was that he did not know the Bible very well. My brother DJ and I would laugh every time he misquoted a scripture. One particular Sunday he was preaching about Lazarus. And he misinterpreted the scripture as implying that Moreover was the name of the dog that licked Lazarus' wounds. As he went on and on about it, the church erupted in laughter. He was angrier than an alligator with long arms. At least my brother and I were actually listening to a sermon for once. After that Sunday, his resentment for our congregation would lead to the great rebellion. Well, that and the Ronnie Jones incident. The Ronnie Jones incident happened while we were attending the" Assembly of Spirit-filled Sanctuaries" convocation or "ASS" as we kids called it. I guess no one had the foresight to see that acronym coming. Our church rented a charter van to Dallas with all the bells and whistles. We were about to join a new convocation. There was not enough room on the bus for all of us so Rev. Johnson decided to drive DJ, Ronnie and Mike (another random kid in our church) to Dallas in his new car. This was the best idea yet because it meant no adults to shut us up. Rev. Al turned out to be a pretty nice dude after all (after he had talked about darn near everybody in the church). The first day of convocation turned out to be like the last ones we attended. There was nothing new but the faces. It was just like the

Baptist convocation. The men spent their days chasing women and the women shopped all day buying elaborate hats, purses and dresses. Then, there was the main event, the opening night musical was like the Grammy Awards on steroids. The air was filled with the aroma of fresh hats and gator skins. The pastors and their wives strolled down the aisles to church VIP like it was the red carpet. And the musicians and singers, that was an entirely different spectacle to behold. It was like an episode of the Oprah show, "you get a neon rayon shirt, you get a neon rayon shirt, everybody gets a neon rayon shirt. "I think I went blind in the first ten minutes of the musical. After the big show, we all went to eat at an all-night restaurant. We were exhausted but we were having a great time. We retreated to our hotel room where all the kids stayed with Rev. Al. The next morning, I was awaken by the sound of crying. It was Ronnie in the bathroom sobbing. I asked him to step outside and tell me what was wrong. He told me that Rev. Al had touched him. I said, well, he touched me too what's wrong with that? He said, no, he touched me, touched me. By that time, Rev. Al had awaken along with the other two boys and said it was time to go to breakfast and then convocation class. Ronnie swore me to secrecy. However, that was like asking me to not eat breakfast. I can't hold water my mother would always say. She was right. After class, I told Mike, DJ, cousin Regina, Cousin Kathy and my momma what Ronnie said? My mother came to our room and told us to pack up because she was getting us our own room. Rev. Al seemed to be genuinely surprised by all this moving around. My mother never accused him of anything for some reason and I would only learn why later. After the commotion, we all attended the grand "Moderator's coronation." This is where the grandest and best preacher in the south was crowned leader of the assembly. They called him "Handsome Harry Barksdale" and he was the grandest of them all. Nope, no question about it, he was playing quarterback for the other team. He was also married with children as well. But, he was also so gifted at preaching and singing no one would dare mention it. To the surprise of everyone, he rejected the nomination of Moderator and stated my father should hold the office. You could hear a pin drop it was quite in the convention center. We were so proud of my father that night but there was an atom bomb staying at the Hilton that was highly upset. Rev. Al had just been suspected of one of the most heinous crimes a person can commit. And then, my father got a position that everyone knew he wanted badly. The next day, he left for Houston without the kids that rode to Dallas with him. We all had to sit with adults on the charter bus. I sat next to Sherry Butler. I do not need to tell you what she smelled like. Whelp, she did smell bad. My father was happy and worried at the same time. He knew this would be trouble when we got back to Houston. He was right. We soon learned that Ronnie and his mother were clinically diagnosed with mental disorders. Making up elaborate illusions was part of their mental illness. However, this did not help to ease Rev. Al's mind. He was a pedophile in the minds of everyone in the church but somehow it was my fathers' fault in his eyes. This was even though no one had actually accused him of anything. My parents gave him the benefit of the doubt and decided to talk to him after we had made it back to town. When our bus arrived, there was Lester and Gena at the church packing up their instruments and Rev. Al was there cheering them on. It was an unholy mess that day. Rev. Al even took a swing at my father but missed. Deacon Haynes (ex-boxer) stepped in and knocked Rev. Al smooth out. But the damage was done. It was over. Rev. Al decided to start his own church and guess who left with him? Lester and Gena took half of the choir (the good singers at that) and Al took half of the congregation. This was the worst day in the history of our church. This was all over an accusation made by a mentally ill kid and his loony mother. I would never forgive Ronnie for what he done. I know now that it was his illness that led him to do what he did, but it was done. I've never seen my father so hurt in all my days. The next Sunday, most of the messy members all came to church asking questions. The story had changed so much, I didn't even remember what actually happened. The stories ranged from Rev. Al was caught sleeping with a hooker, to my dad had stabbed Rev. Al and anything you can think of in between. Our church membership would eventually drop from over 600 to about 200 members. The worst part is that people who had been loyal members were now convinced that my father was somehow an unfair brawler. Any preacher's kid will tell you that it hurts deep when people speak ill of their parents. Especially when no one acknowledges the sacrifices they make for their members. I guess Rev. Al forgot about all the times my father paid his rent when he was unemployed for 2 years. Or did he forget that when his mother had cancer my father took care of her with his own money? Or did he forget that his brand new car was bought with money the church paid him for half-painting the church? Maybe, he also forgot that his grandma didn't have life insurance and the church raised money to pay for her burial. These are things my father would never mention that he did for members through the years. He gave away new suits, money, time and once a car just because that's who he was. He never asked anyone for anything but to love God like he does. Still, they betrayed him for their own reasons. My parents taught all five of us forgiveness. There were times I never understood how they could possibly forgive some of the awful things people said about them and did to them, until now.

CHAPTER 5:
TROUBLE WITH THE SPLITTER

It is now 1989 and I'm about to graduate high school. I spent most of the first part of my senior year worried about my parents and my church home. To be honest, I was very angry. Now I was old enough to not hold back and tell these preachers how I really felt about them. Unlike my father and my brother, my filter was broken and I liked it that way. One day I saw Rev. Al at our neighborhood convenience store. He actually smiled, spoke to me and then proceeded to ask me how my parents were doing. What happened next cannot ever be repeated. Just know I was a pretty good curser at that stage of my life. I then ended the conversation by saying, "I hope you drop dead." The next week my mother woke my father up to tell him that Rev. Al was trampled by a herd of wild elephants. Well, not exactly, he had a heart-attack and died suddenly. I guess I was really the biggest prophet in the house after all.

Normally I would have been shaken after wishing death upon someone and then it happens. Not this time. When a church splits, no one wins. Most of the time, it's because of a preacher that thinks (in his mind) that he is better than the pastor that's already established. I call it, "Assistant-Preacher-Selfishness-Syndrome" or ASS. That acronym keeps rearing its ugly head. Well, that's exactly what they are, a group of selfish, horses-assess. They are worse than the bootleg preachers because they at least have the decency to hide their true "self." The great poet Nas once remarked, "You are who you are best when no one is looking." But assistant preachers lurk in the shadows. They despise the light because they have ill-motives. They pretend to be loyal and fain dedication. All the while they are lusting for power like a young lion. When they disagree with the leader, they not only leave the church but they take with them like-minded, weak people. There is nothing more harmful, no cancerous, to a ministry than a church that has been split. Kelvin Dollar knew this very important fact first hand. One of his young ASS preachers had taken 250 of his best members, his musicians and $5000 along with him two years ago. He heard about our church troubles (so did the entire city) and told my father he was coming to help. That's exactly what he did too. He preached a sermon titled, "A house divided cannot stand." My father announced this service on the radio. So, of course, all of the messy people returned for this service just to hear what he was going to say. Even Lester and Gena returned to hear the sermon. But it wasn't exactly a sermon. He basically put everyone who had left on blast and reminded them of the man my father truly was. He called the roll for about two hours reminding folks of just how my father had done all of the amazing things for pastors, deacons, choir members, homeless people, sick people and all kinds of people. "Shame on you, shame on you, shame on you," he decried and repeated! There was not a dry eye in the church. People were crying, repenting and apologizing for weeks after that sermon. And the people began to slowly come back to the fold. Even people my father didn't want back returned. Rev. Dollar had did it. His kind efforts never went unnoticed by my family either. He and my father would remain friends until the day Dollar closed his eyes and went home to meet Preacher-Jesus. You will meet a wealth of preachers during your lifetime but you will call very few "friend." Fortunately, my father found out this concept very early in his ministry. The burning question that I had was how could he continue to get duped so many times by so many preachers? Did he have a need for pain?

The answer to those questions lie in another type of split. During my father's teen-age years, his mother and father separated. Consequently, he felt abandoned by his father. He was forced to be his own man and find his own way through life. But, he was old school and country. If you know anything about country people, they are "trusting." Some would say to a fault.

He took a man's word as his bond. Unfortunately, city men don't always adhere to the same set of rules of engagement. He was used by preachers that were very adapted to surviving by lurking in the shadows. He was prey to them. Now, he was forced to grow up in God and lean heavily on himself and only a handful of close clergymen. That was a recipe that would serve him well. It is now 1991 and Jackson Hammond heard the voice of God tell him to build himself his very own grand cathedral. But that my friends, is the next book. Stay tuned.

www.ingramcontent.com/pod-product-compliance
Lightning Source LLC
Chambersburg PA
CBHW051311170626
46809CB00004B/1854